Dinorella

A Prehistoric Fairy Tale

PAMELA DUNCAN EDWARDS

HENRY COLE

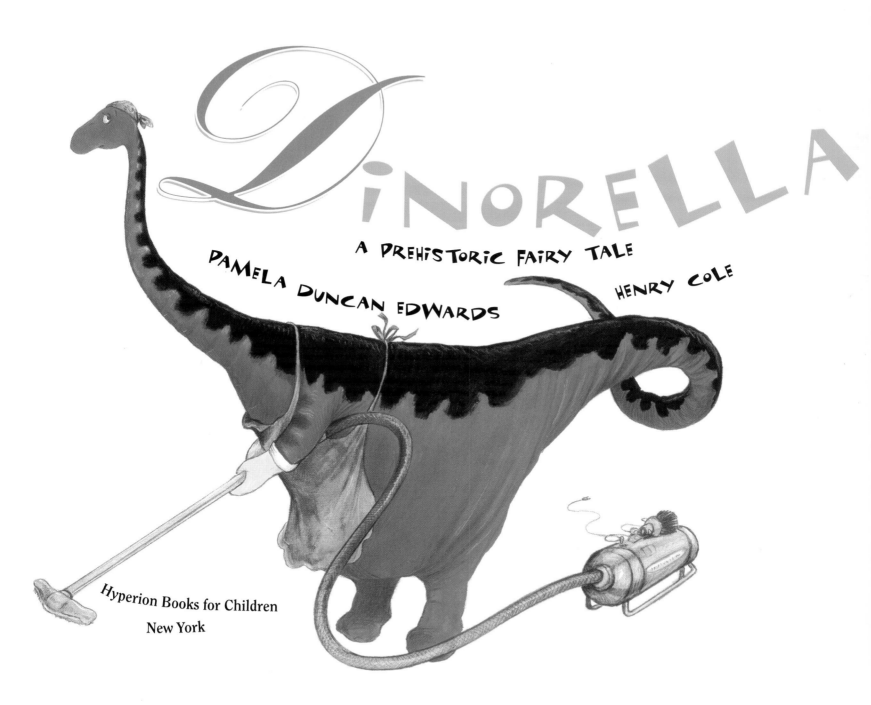

Hyperion Books for Children
New York

FOR JULIE AND ROBERT,
A DARLING DUO
—P. D. E.

TO LYNDI,
MY PINKY-PACT PAL
—H. C.

Text © 1997 by Pamela Duncan Edwards.
Illustrations © 1997 by Henry Cole.

Printed in the United States of America.

FIRST EDITION
1 3 5 7 9 10 8 6 4 2

The artwork for each picture is prepared using acrylic paints and
colored pencils on Arches Hot Press watercolor paper.
This book is set in 18-point Clearface Heavy.

Library of Congress Cataloging-in-Publication Data
Edwards, Pamela Duncan.
Dinorella / Pamela Duncan Edwards ; illustrated by Henry Cole. —
1st ed.
p.   cm.
Summary: In this story, loosely based on that of Cinderella but
featuring dinosaurs, the duke falls in love with Dinorella when she
rescues him from the dreaded deinonychus at the Dinosaur Dance.
ISBN 0-7868-0309-6 (trade)—ISBN 0-7868-2249-X (lib. bdg.)
[1. Dinosaurs—Fiction. 2. Humorous stories.] I. Cole, Henry,
ill. II. Title.
PZ7.E26365Di   1997   96-38542

Dora, Doris, and Dinorella lived down in the
sand dunes in a dinosaur den.

Dora and Doris did nothing all day. They dumped debris
around the den. They never did the dusting or the dishes.
Dinorella was dainty and dependable. Dora and Doris
were dreadful to Dinorella. All day they demanded . . .

"DiNORELLA, dig the garden.

"DiNORELLA, fetch us drinks.

"DiNORELLA, start the dinner."

"She's a dingbat," sniggered Dora.
"She's a dumbhead," giggled Doris.

One day a card was delivered to the den:

Dinosaur Dance
Duke Dudley's Den
At Dusk
Hors d'oeuvres, Dandelion Cola
Dancing Until Dawn

Duke Dudley was the most dashing dinosaur in the dunes.

"I would die for a date with the duke," said Dora, decorating herself with dinosaur jewels.

"Definitely," sighed Doris, dolling up for the dance.

"A dance," said Dinorella diffidently, "How divine."

"YOU can't go to the dance," said Doris. "YOU'RE too dowdy."

"YOU'RE too dull," agreed Dora. "And YOU don't have decent dinosaur jewels. Of course YOU can't go to the dance."

Poor Dinorella felt down in the dumps as she watched her stepsisters depart.

Suddenly, Dinorella heard a droning noise.

"Don't be dismal," cried Fairydactyl.

"You **SHALL** go to the dance."

"But I'm so drab," said Dinorella,

"and I don't have decent dinosaur jewels."

"I'll soon deal with that," declared Fairydactyl.

"These will outdazzle all other dinosaur jewels."

"**DARLING** Fairydactyl!" exclaimed Dinorella in delight.

With her diamonds dangling, she set out for the dance.

Dusk had fallen when Dinorella heard a deafening
disturbance coming from the direction of
Duke Dudley's Den.

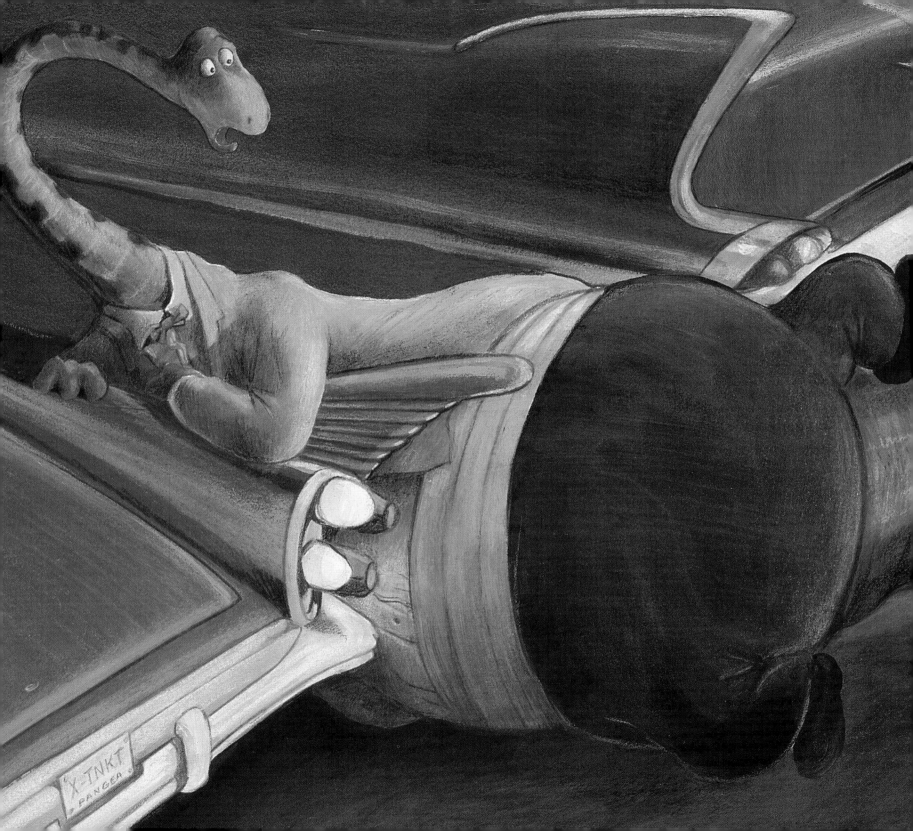

A DASTARDLY DEED WAS TAKING PLACE!

A deinonychus was dragging off the duke.
"I'M DONE FOR!" cried the duke.
"He will DEVOUR me!"
"Indeed I will!" laughed the deinonychus.
"I'll be digesting you by daybreak."

Dinorella was not a daring dinosaur,
but something drastic had to be done.
"I may become dessert, but I'm determined to drive away
that dreaded carnivore."
Dinorella climbed to the top of the dune.
"YOU DISGUSTING DUMMY," she roared.
"DROP THE DUKE!"
Dinorella began to hurl dirtballs at the deinonychus.

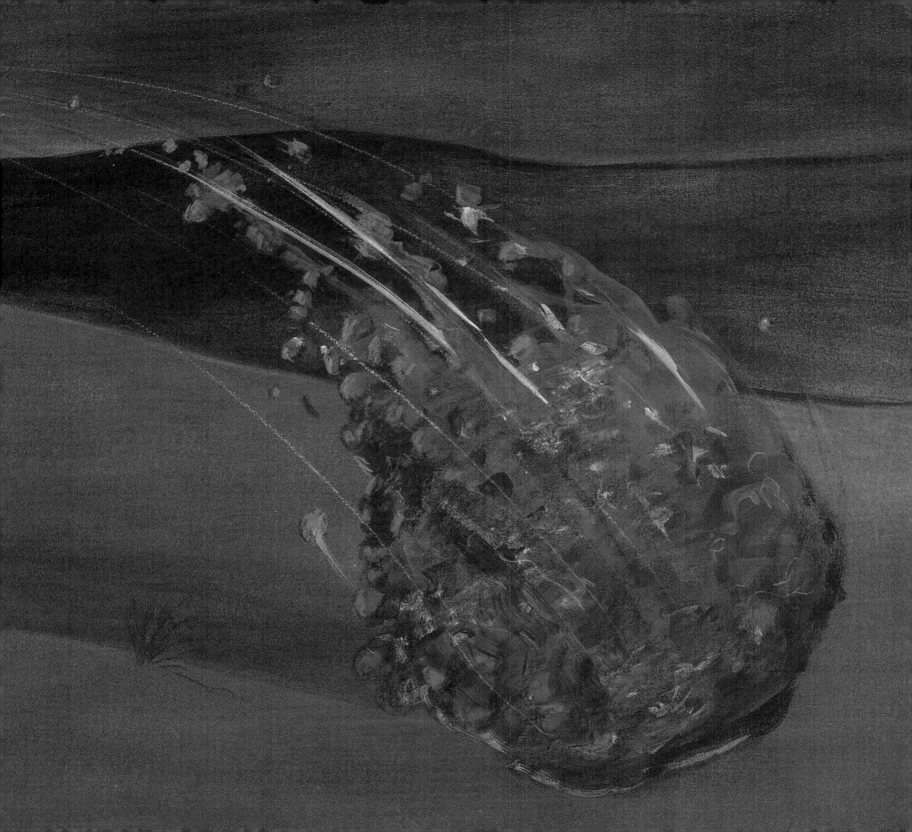

The dumbfounded deinonychus stopped in disbelief.
"Who called me a dummy?" he demanded.
The moon's light caught Dinorella's dangling diamonds. Dots and dabs of light darted toward the deinonychus.

"A DEVIL!" cried the deinonychus.
"See its dreadful demon eyes!"

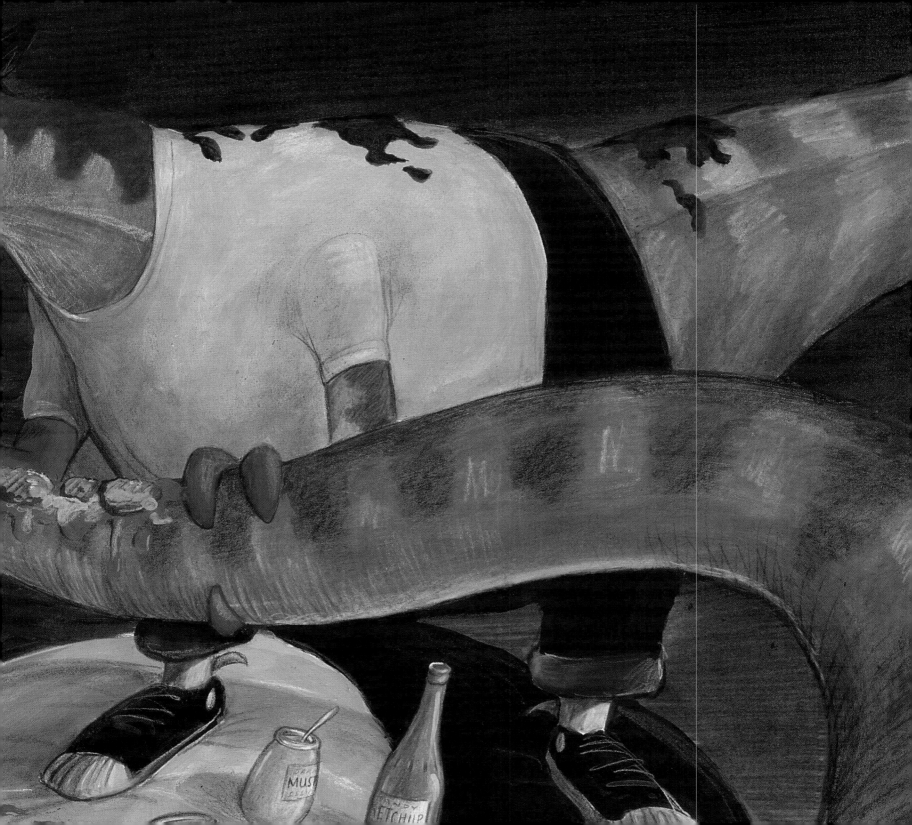

Dinorella detached a diamond and directed it toward the deinonychus.
The diamond hit the deinonychus **HARD** in his dentures.

"The devil will destroy me with its deadly eyes,"
bellowed the distraught deinonychus.
He dumped Duke Dudley and departed
double-quick.

The den was dense with dinosaurs dashing about in distress. "A demon," they cried. "We're **DOOMED**." "**DIMWITS!**" roared Duke Dudley through the din. "Demons don't throw diamonds. It was a damsel who defended me with her dazzling dinosaur jewel.

"When I discover her,
I shall ask her to be my darling."

All the dinosaur dames were delirious.
"The jewel is mine!" they each declared.

"MINE!" cried Doris.

"NO, DEFINITELY MINE,"
bellowed Dora, giving Doris a dig.
"I am the damsel you desire."

"I DOUBT IT,"
declared Duke Dudley.
"Your dinosaur jewels don't match."

Just then, Fairydactyl arrived at the dance.
She quickly saw the dilemma.
"WHERE IS DINORELLA?" she demanded.
"Dinorella!" scoffed Dora, "that dopey domestic."
"Dinorella!" laughed Doris. "She's back at the den."
But Fairydactyl spied Dinorella dodging behind the dune.
"DINORELLA," she directed, "come down."
So down came Dinorella, looking distracted.
Cried the duke, "She wears but one dazzling jewel!"

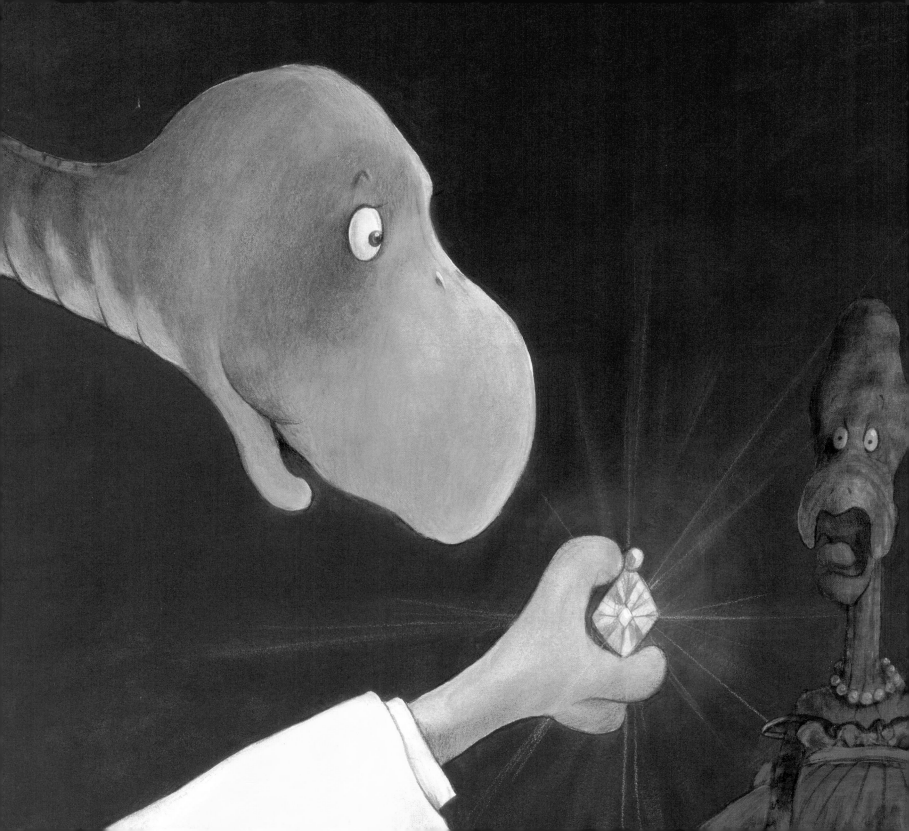

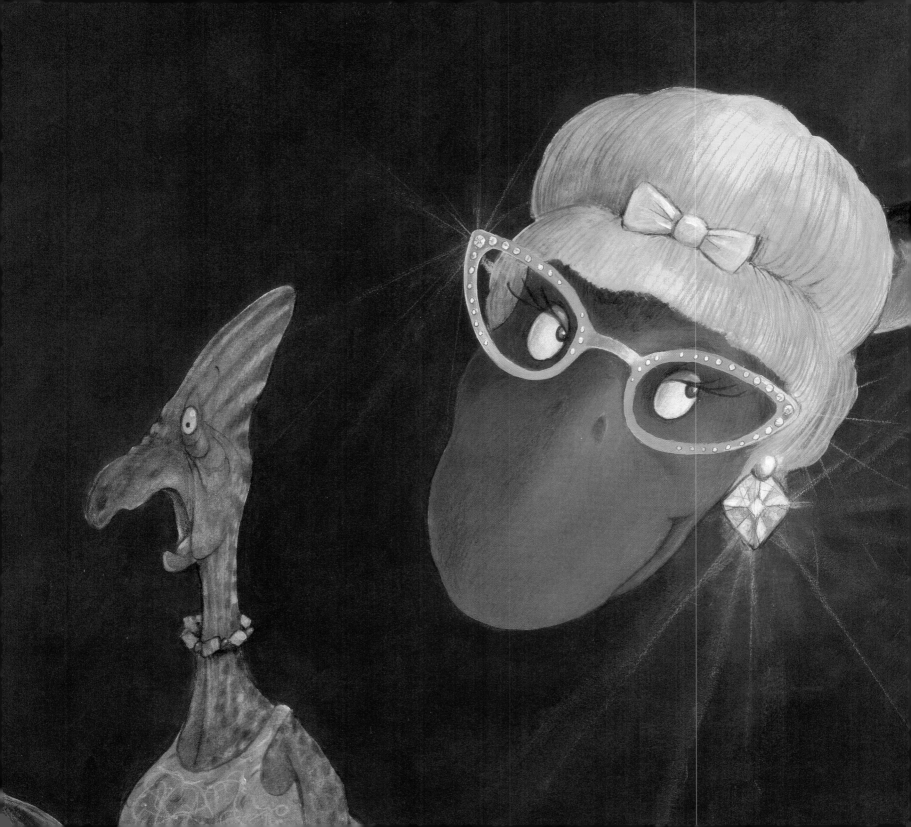

"Dinorella, you are adorable. You're definitely quite a dish. I beg you to be my dearest."

"DRAT!" said Dora and Doris.